For Mum

Speedy Goes to School

小快上學去

Jill McDougall 著

王祖民 繪

"Come on, Speedy," said Julie. "You have to come to school."

Julie took her *pet turtle out of his *tank and put him in a box.

Then she took him to school.

*為生字，請參照生字表

"We are learning about *reptiles," said Mrs. Ma. "Vic will show us his pet snake and Julie will show us her pet turtle."

Vic was first. He had a snake around his neck.

"This is Sam," he said. "He likes to eat rats and mice."

"Does he eat turtles?" asked Julie.

"*Maybe," said Vic.

"Oh dear," said Julie.

Julie was next. She held up her box.

"My pet turtle is in here," she said.

She put her hand in the box.

Speedy was not there!

"Speedy has run away," cried Julie.

"Oh dear," said Mrs. Ma.

Mr. Chen came into the room.

"What is wrong?" he asked.

"My turtle has run away," said Julie.

"Oh dear," said Mr. Chen.

Then he jumped up and down.

"There is something on my leg," he cried.

Julie looked. Was it Speedy?

No, it was only an ant.

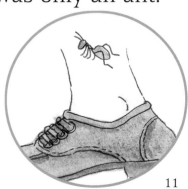

Then Mrs. Ma jumped up and down.

"There is something behind the chair," she cried.

Julie looked. Was it Speedy?

No, it was only Vic's snake, Sam.

Then Vic jumped up and down. "Look at Sam!" he cried.

Everyone looked at Vic's snake. He had a very fat *belly.

"Oh dear," said Mr. Chen.

"Oh dear," said Mrs. Ma.

"Oh dear," said Vic.

Julie felt very sad. She *patted Sam's fat belly.

"Good-bye, Speedy," she said.

"Take out your pencils," said Mrs. Ma. "We will draw some reptile pictures."

"I'll draw a snake," said a boy.

"I'll draw a *dinosaur," said a girl.

"I'll draw Speedy," said Julie, sadly.

She looked in her bag. Her red pen was in there.
Something *else was in there, too.

Speedy!

Just then, Vic said, "I've lost my Mickey Mouse pencil case."

"Oh dear," said Mrs. Ma.

Everyone looked for the pencil case. They looked under the chairs. They looked under the tables. They looked behind the books. They looked in the trash can.

No pencil case.

Then Julie had an idea. She looked at Vic's snake.

He seemed to be *smiling. She looked at his fat belly.

"Oh dear," she said.

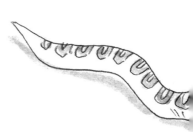

生字表

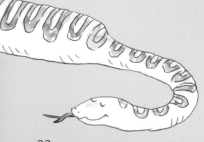

adv.= 副詞， n.= 名詞， v.= 動詞

p.2
茱莉說：「來吧！小快。你得到學校去。」
茱莉將她的寵物烏龜從飼養箱中拿出來，放進一個盒子裡，然後帶著他到學校去。

p.4-5
馬老師說：「我們要來認識爬蟲類。維克會讓我們看看他的寵物蛇，茱莉則會讓我們看看她的寵物烏龜。」

維克先開始。他的脖子上繞著一條蛇。
他說：「這是山姆，他喜歡吃大老鼠和小老鼠。」
茱莉問：「他會吃烏龜嗎？」
維克說：「也許吧。」
茱莉說：「喔！天啊！」

p.6
接下來輪到茱莉了。
她把她的盒子舉起來說：「我的寵物烏龜就在裡面。」
她把手伸進盒子裡。
小快不在裡面！
茱莉大叫：「小快跑掉了！」
馬老師說：「喔！天啊！」

p.8

大家都在找小快。他們往椅子下找；他們往桌子下找；他們往書的後面找；他們往垃圾桶裡找。
都沒有小快的蹤影。

p.10-11

陳老師走進教室裡。
他問：「怎麼了？」
茱莉說：「我的烏龜跑掉了！」
陳老師說：「喔！天啊！」接著他上上下下的跳了起來，大叫說：「我的腿上有東西！」
茱莉看了看，會是小快嗎？
不是，那只是隻螞蟻。

p.12

接著，換馬老師上上下下的跳了起來，大叫說：「椅子後面有東西！」
茱莉看了看，會是小快嗎？
不是，那只是維克的蛇，山姆。

p.14-15

然後，這次換維克上上下下的跳了起來，大叫說：「快看山姆！」

大家都看著維克的蛇。他的肚子又肥又大。

陳老師說：「喔！天啊！」

馬老師說：「喔！天啊！」

維克說：「喔！天啊！」

茉莉覺得好傷心。她拍拍山姆肥肥的肚子說：「再見了，小快。」

p.16-17

馬老師說：「把你們的鉛筆拿出來，我們來畫爬蟲類。」

有一個男生說：「我要畫蛇。」

有一個女生說：「我要畫恐龍。」

茉莉難過的說：「我要畫小快。」她往她的袋子裡看，她的紅筆在裡面。還有另一樣東西也在裡面。是小快！

25

p.18-19

就在這個時候，維克說：「我的米老鼠鉛筆盒不見了。」
馬老師說：「喔！天啊！」
大家都在找維克的鉛筆盒。
他們往椅子下找；他們往桌子下找；他們往書的後面找；他們往垃圾桶裡找。
都沒有看到鉛筆盒。

p.20

然後茱莉想到了一件事。她看看維克的蛇，他好像在微笑。她又看看他肥肥的肚子，然後說：「喔！天啊！」

句型轉換練習

(2) There is a green bag on the desk.
There is a red book under the desk.
There is a blue book between the chairs.
There is a red book behind the boy.

句型練習

There's Something....

在「小快上學去」故事中，出現了很多有關 "There is (something)...." （[某處] 有……）的用法，現在我們就一起來練習這個句型吧！

1 請跟著 CD 的 Track 4，唸出下面這些介系詞：

behind the chair

before the chair

by the desk

on the chair

under the chair

between the chairs

There is something on my leg.

There is something behind the chair.

There is something in Sam's belly.

What do you see in the picture?

There is a green bag _____ the desk.

There is a red book _____ the desk.

There is a blue book _____ the chairs.

There is a red book _____ the boy.

認識爬蟲類（Reptile）

　　你有去過動物園裡的爬蟲館嗎？除了故事中提到的烏龜和蛇以外，你知道還有哪些動物屬於爬蟲類嗎？牠們的特徵又是什麼？現在就讓我們簡單的認識一下，什麼叫做爬蟲類。

　　「爬蟲類」這三個字裡雖然有「蟲」字，但是這些動物跟昆蟲可是完全不一樣的生物喔！像烏龜、蛇、鱷魚、蜥蜴、壁虎、變色龍、還有絕種很久的恐龍等等，都屬於爬蟲類。

★ 爬蟲類有哪些特性？

1. 皮膚：爬蟲類通常具有厚而乾燥的皮膚，如蛇、蜥蜴等；或是硬梆梆的外殼，如烏龜，讓牠們能夠保留住體內的水分。這麼一來，牠們就可以遠離水源、深入陸地生活。

2. 四肢：除了沒有腳的蛇以外，爬蟲類大多擁有強壯的四肢，讓牠們在面對草原與森林裡各式各樣的危機與敵人時，能夠生存下來，或為自己搶得食物。

3. 體溫：爬蟲類是「變溫性動物」，也有人稱呼牠們為「冷血動物」，也就是說，牠們的體溫會隨著週遭的環境變化，一但生活環境溫度太高或太低，牠們就會移到溫度比較適中的地區，來調節體溫。此外，在天氣較冷的地區，爬蟲類的行動會變得遲緩、甚至無法行動，所以有冬眠的習性。

4. 嘴巴：爬蟲類嘴巴附近的關節是可以調整移動的，所以能夠把嘴巴張得很大很大，用來吞掉獵物。

★ 爬蟲類怎麼繁衍後代？

　　大部分的爬蟲類都是卵生，不過只有少數爬蟲類會孵蛋。蛋的數量、大小跟孵出來的時間，會因為種類不同而相異，例如故事中的紅耳龜小快，大概要花三個月的時間才會「破蛋而出」。

　　現在對爬蟲類了解了這麼多，下回去動物園時，記得去拜訪這些奇特又有趣的生物喔！

寫書的人

Jill McDougall is an Australian children's writer whose first book, "Anna the Goanna," was a Children's Book Council Notable Book. Jill has written and published over eighty titles for children including short stories, picture books and novels. Jill enjoys yoga, cooking and walking her two dogs along the beach.

畫畫的人

　　王祖民，江蘇蘇州市人。現任江蘇少年兒童出版社美術編輯副編審，從事兒童讀物插圖創作工作，作品曾多次在國際國內獲獎。作品《虎丘山》曾獲聯合國科教文野間兒童讀物插圖獎。

小烏龜大麻煩系列
Turtle Trouble Series

Jill McDougall 著／王祖民 繪

附中英雙語朗讀CD／適合具基礎英文閱讀能力者(國小4-6年級)閱讀

① 貪吃的烏龜小快 (Speedy the Greedy Turtle)　④ 電視明星小快 (Speedy the TV Star)

② 小快的比賽 (Speedy's Race)　⑤ 怎麼啦，小快？ (What's Wrong, Speedy?)

③ 小快上學去 (Speedy Goes to School)　⑥ 小快在哪裡？ (Where Is Speedy?)

　　烏龜小快是小女孩茱莉養的寵物，他既懶散又貪吃，還因此鬧出不少笑話，讓茱莉一家人的生活充滿歡笑跟驚奇！想知道烏龜小快發生了什麼事嗎？快看《小烏龜大麻煩系列》故事，保證讓你笑聲不斷喔！

活潑可愛的插畫
還有突破傳統的編排方式
視覺效果令人耳目一新

幽默的文字，簡單的句型，
不會造成閱讀負擔

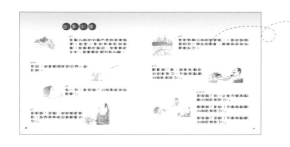

故事中譯保持英文原味，又可當成
完整的中文故事閱讀

書後附英文句型練習，加強讀者應
用句型能力，幫助讀者融會貫通

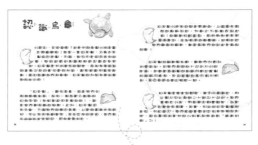

補充與故事有關的小常識，讓讀者
更了解故事內容

附英文生字表，幫助讀者了解故事內容

小老鼠貝貝歷險記系列
Tabitha and the Elephants

Marc Ponomareff　著／王平，倪靖，郜欣　繪／本局編輯部　譯

精裝／附中英雙語朗讀CD／全套六本

一隻機智勇敢的小老鼠，一隻真誠可愛的象寶寶，
六本為孩子量身打造的雙語繪本，
讓你在一連串驚險刺激的冒險故事中學英文！

① Tabitha Meets An Elephant　　　　貝貝與小潔的相遇
② Tabitha and the Laughing Hyenas　小老鼠貝貝與土狼
③ Tabitha and the Python　　　　　小老鼠貝貝與大蟒蛇
④ Tabitha and the Crocodile　　　　小老鼠貝貝與鱷魚
⑤ Tabitha Escapes from the Lions　　小老鼠貝貝逃生記
⑥ A Party for Tabitha　　　　　　小老鼠貝貝的驚喜派對

國家圖書館出版品預行編目資料

Speedy Goes to School:小快上學去 / Jill McDougall
著;王祖民繪;本局編輯部譯.－－初版一刷.－－臺
北市：三民，2005
　　面；　公分.－－(Fun心讀雙語叢書.小烏龜，大
麻煩系列③)
中英對照
ISBN 957-14-4324-7　（精裝）
1. 英國語言－讀本

523.38　　　　　　　　　　　　　　　94012415

網路書店位址　http://www.sanmin.com.tw

© **Speedy Goes to School**
——小快上學去

著作人　Jill McDougall
繪　者　王祖民
譯　者　本局編輯部
發行人　劉振強
著作財　三民書局股份有限公司
產權人　臺北市復興北路386號
發行所　三民書局股份有限公司
　　　　地址／臺北市復興北路386號
　　　　電話／(02)25006600
　　　　郵撥／0009998-5
印刷所　三民書局股份有限公司
門市部　復北店／臺北市復興北路386號
　　　　重南店／臺北市重慶南路一段61號
初版一刷　2005年8月
編　號　S 805601
定　價　新臺幣壹佰捌拾元整
行政院新聞局登記證局版臺業字第○二○○號

ISBN　957-14-4324-7　（精裝）